A Desert Trek

Acknowledgments

Executive Editor: Diane Sharpe
Supervising Editor: Stephanie Muller
Design Manager: Sharon Golden
Page Design: Simon Balley Design Associates
Photography: Bruce Coleman: cover (top right, bottom right), pages 9, 15, 17, 23, 25, 27; NHPA: pages 15, 21, 27; Science Photo Library: page 11; Tony Stone: cover (middle right), page 13.

ISBN 0-8114-3796-5

Copyright © 1995 Steck-Vaughn Company.

1 2 3 4 5 6 7 8 9 00 PO 00 99 98 97 96 95 94

A
Desert
Trek

Mike Herschell

Illustrated by
Peter Bull

STECK-VAUGHN
C O M P A N Y
ELEMENTARY • SECONDARY • ADULT • LIBRARY

4

Why did we have to wait all day before beginning our trek?

Because it is much cooler in the evening.

The desert gets very hot during the day. In the morning and evening, it is much cooler. At night it can be very cold.

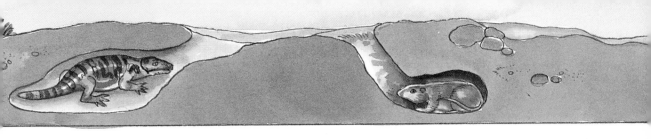

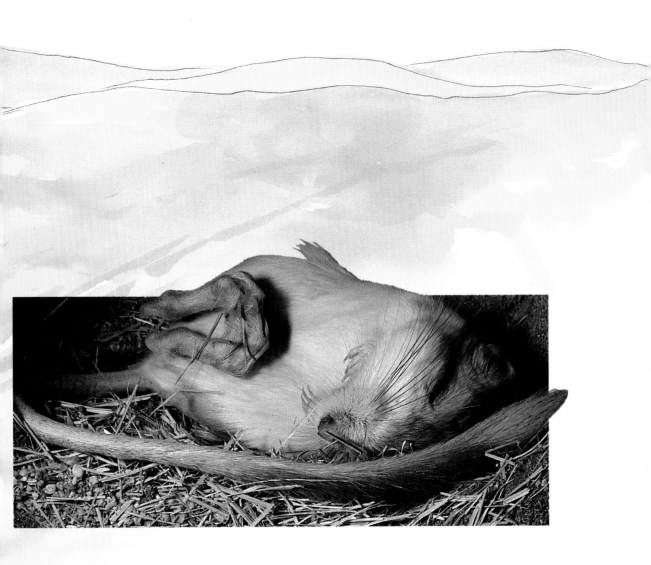

During the day, many desert animals
hide from the hot sun. They stay in
burrows or under rocks and come
out in the evening or at night.

These rock towers are made when
wind and sand wear away the soft
rock on the outside. This leaves the
hard rock standing.

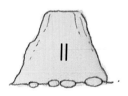

It is a giant cactus. It grows very
slowly and can live for 250 years.

14

The gila woodpecker makes its nest by carving out a hole in the side of the giant cactus.

There's another bird running across the sand!

That's a roadrunner.

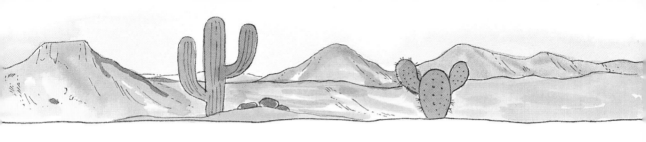

The roadrunner is a kind of cuckoo.
But it doesn't lay its eggs in other birds'
nests like cuckoos do. The roadrunner can
fly, but it usually runs along the ground.

17

The ant lion is an insect. It digs a little
hole in the sand and then buries itself at
the bottom. When other insects fall into
the hole, the ant lion catches them and
eats them.

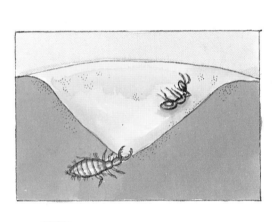

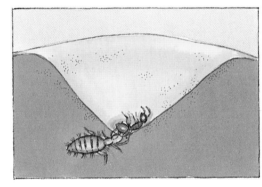

The horned lizard is camouflaged so that it looks like the rocks and sand.

The horned lizard is one of many reptiles living in the desert. Its scaly skin keeps it from drying out in the sun.

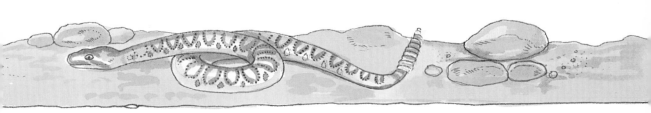

Rattlesnakes are shy animals that hide away
in the rocks. They are very poisonous.
They may attack people if they are disturbed
in any way.

Kangaroo rats have long back legs,
just like kangaroos. They can jump
up as high as your head.

25

They wake up when we go to bed.

It's your bedtime now and time to get back to camp.

Kit Fox

Coyote

Look at this picture. How many desert plants and animals can you remember? The answers are on the last page, but don't look until you have tried naming everything.

29

The plants and animals in this book are shown at different sizes than they really are. This is how big they are compared to you.

Gila woodpecker

Ant lion

Horned lizard

Kangaroo rat

Roadrunner

Rattlesnake

Kit fox

Coyote

Index

Ant lion **18-19, 28, 30**
Arizona **4**

Burrows **9**

Camouflage **21**
Coyotes **26-27, 28**
Cuckoo **17**

Desert park **4**

Giant cactus **12-13, 14-15, 29**
Gila woodpecker **14-15, 29, 30**

Horned lizard **20-21, 29, 30**

Kangaroo rat **24-25, 28, 30**
Kit fox **26-27, 28**

Nighttime **7, 9, 24, 26**

Poisonous **23**

Rattlesnake **22-23, 28**
Reptile **21**
Roadrunner **16-17, 29**
Rock towers **10-11**

Temperature **6-7, 9**

Answers: 1. Coyote 2. Rattlesnake 3. Kangaroo rat 4. Kit fox 5. Ant lion
6. Giant cactus 7. Gila woodpecker 8. Roadrunner 9. Horned lizard